Screw Loose

by

Alison Prince

Illustrated by Alison Prince

You do not need to read this page - just get on with the book!

Published in 2002 in Great Britain by
Barrington Stoke Ltd
10 Belford Terrace, Edinburgh EH4 3DQ

This edition based on *Screw Loose*, published by Barrington Stoke in 1999

Printed by Polestar AUP Aberdeen Ltd

MEET THE AUTHOR AND ILLUSTRATOR - ALISON PRINCE

What is your favourite animal?
My cats, Charlie and Jessica

What is your favourite boy's name?
Cosmo

What is your favourite girl's name?
Philomena

What is your favourite food?
Home-made bread

What is your favourite music?
Mozart and jazz

What is your favourite hobby?
Playing the clarinet

To all those who have ever wished
things were different

Contents

Chapter 1
The Screwdriver

Roddy found the screwdriver by the school gate. It was a short, strong screwdriver, just the right size to fit into his pocket.

He tried it out on a hook in the cloakroom. It came off with no bother at all. Roddy smiled and put the screwdriver back in his pocket. Then he went on up to his classroom. He was late. He was always late.

"Roddy, you're late," said his teacher, Mrs Bigg.

"Yes, Miss," Roddy nodded. "Sorry."

"Why are you always late?" asked Mrs Bigg.

"Dunno," said Roddy.

Why did she have to ask? You'd have to be mad to want to come into school for the whole day. Boring, boring. No way. It was better to hang about a bit on the way to school. He could go into the corner shop before he got on the bus and get some crisps and gum.

But now he had the screwdriver. That would make school more fun.

"I might be early tomorrow," he said.

"Oh, good," said Mrs Bigg.

3

Next day, Roddy was in school before anyone else. He used the screwdriver to take off the notice on the Head's door and the catch on the two windows.

Then he took the hinges off the door of the boys' toilet. He had a go at the brackets that held up the shelves in his classroom.

He had just started to work on the tables when the door opened and Biff came in.

She had a stack of magazines in her arms. "Hi," she said. "Why are you so early?"

"Oh, I just am," said Roddy. "Why are you early?"

"My mum works at the hospital," Biff said. "She's a cleaner. She has to go in early. I go with her. That's where I get all the mags. The nurse chucks out all the old ones."

She put the mags on a table. It tipped up as one of its legs gave way.

Roddy tried to look as if all this was nothing to do with him.

"The leg's come off," he said as he picked the table up. He took the screwdriver out of his pocket and hoped Biff would not see that the screws were in there as well. But she did, of course.

"So that's why you were in so early," she said. "Hey, was it you who undid the KNOCK AND WAIT notice off the Head's door? I saw it lying on the floor."

"Could be," said Roddy.

Biff smiled. "Great!" she said. "Wait till I tell Debbie and Sheena!"

"Don't go telling everyone," said Roddy. "If the jannie finds out, I'm dead."

"What's a jannie?" asked someone from the door.

Roddy and Biff looked round. Tim Tomkins was standing there. Tim had just come up to Scotland from London. He didn't know anything yet.

"A jannie's a janitor," Biff told him. "He looks after the school, does the boilers and that sort of thing."

"Is Mr Rundle the jannie?" asked Tim. "Hangs out in that little office near the bogs?"

"That's right," said Roddy.

"So what must he not find out?" Tim asked.

"Nothing," said Biff and Roddy together.

Tim nodded. Then he went over to his place and sat down. He looked so sad that they told him about the screwdriver.

Roddy said he'd wreck his Game Boy if he let on.

Chapter 2
Mr Rundle

Everyone was standing round the chip van at lunch. Roddy went into the boys' toilet to unscrew a few more things.
He found Mr Rundle putting back the hinges on the door.

"You should be outside," said Mr Rundle.

"I need a pee," said Roddy.

"On you go, then."

Roddy didn't need a pee at all, and found it hard to do much with Mr Rundle looking on.

"What's the matter with the door?" Roddy asked.

"Vandals," said Mr Rundle.

"What do you mean?"

Mr Rundle sighed. "Someone around here has been unscrewing things."

"Go on," said Roddy.

Mr Rundle looked at him hard. "I've lost one of my screwdrivers. A short one, with a stubby handle. Have *you* seen it?"

"No!" Roddy said, but his voice sounded odd.

"I want it back," said Mr Rundle.

As Roddy went out, he knew Mr Rundle was staring at him.

After that, unscrewing things was a risky game. But it was still fun. Roddy knew he was giving Mr Rundle a lot of work, but it was great to have something to do in school at last. He couldn't stop now.

When no-one was around, he unscrewed desk legs and took down notice boards. He even got at the framed portrait of some old person who had been the first headteacher of the school. Roddy was proud of this, because the portrait hung just outside the Head's room.

The Head was a thin, stiff man who did not understand jokes. In assembly he would snatch his glasses off and on and run his fingers through his hair.

The Head told everyone that there was a vandal in the school. Roddy was glad the Head had not offered a reward for telling him who the vandals were. If the reward was worth it, someone would have cracked.

Dave Boyle's gang, who did most of the graffiti and damage everywhere, were mad as hell that they had not thought of it first.

Joe Picken came in with a huge great screwdriver but it fell out of his sports bag and he was found out. He got suspended, of course, but he didn't mind. It gave him more time to do his shoplifting.

The Head was even more upset because the unscrewing *still* did not stop.

The Head called in the police to talk to the school at Assembly. The police officer went on and on about how awful it was to start out on a life of crime.

When the Head stepped to the stand to thank the policeman, the top fell off. It hit him on the big toe. He stood there on one foot, trying not to hop, while everyone fell off their chairs laughing. It was one of Roddy's best tricks, and even the police officer was grinning, though he blew his nose to try and hide it.

Chapter 3
Wanted

The next morning, Mr Rundle was waiting in a van outside Roddy's flat.

"They want you," he said through the van's open window. "Get in."

"Want me?" said Roddy.

So the game was up. If you were wanted, it had to mean the police.

"Where are we going?" he asked. He tried to sound calm.

"School, of course. But they asked me to have a word with you first." Mr Rundle started the van and they set off down the road. "You see, the Head's been taken ill."

"What sort of ill?"

"Mental. His wife rang in this morning to say he was under the table, barking like a dog. You've got to take over."

"What d'you mean, take over?" asked Roddy.

"What I say. You're to be the new Head. They had the good sense to come and ask me what to do. I told them they should make *you* Head."

He's having me on, Roddy thought. *Why me?* But at the back of his mind, he knew why.

"I know you, son," Mr Rundle said. "Like they say, you don't have to be mad to be a Head, but it helps. And you've got a screw loose, haven't you?"

Roddy went red. Mr Rundle held out his hand and said, "You'd best give me that screwdriver back. Could be tricky if you were found with it. You being the Head and all."

Roddy fished in his pocket and took out the small screwdriver. He would miss it.

"Thanks," said Mr Rundle, and dropped it into his pocket. "I've missed that."

Roddy nodded. He understood how he felt. "Sorry," he said.

"That's all right." Mr Rundle drove on.

As they came near the school, Roddy said, "Am I dreaming?"

"Maybe," said Mr Rundle. "But I'm not."

Panic hit Roddy. "I can't do this," he said. "Run the school? This is a joke, isn't it?"

"No," said Mr Rundle. "It's not a joke. It may be a silly idea, but it's worth giving it a try."

"But what shall I *do*?" yelled Roddy.

"Anything you like. Just don't sack the teachers. Not yet."

Roddy nodded. He was thinking fast. "Does everyone know I'm in charge?"

"Your name's on the Head's door," said Mr Rundle. "And the staff have been told."

He drove the van into the school car park.

Chapter 4
The Head

Roddy saw his own name on the door of the Head's office.

MR RODERICK WATT, HEADMASTER.

"I shall have to call you Mr Watt in front of the kids," said Mr Rundle.

Roddy went over to the desk and sat down behind it. He felt very small. "What shall I do?" he asked again.

"Call a meeting," Mr Rundle told him. "That's what they all do. If you want to talk to the whole school, press the button on your desk. Then speak into the mike and the whole school will hear you. Best of luck."

He went out, and shut the door behind him.

Roddy spun about in the Head's big chair. He could spin right round if he gave himself a good push off.

The noise was growing outside his window. The whole school was there waiting for the bell to ring. Biff would be in the classroom now, getting her mags set out for a day's reading. Tim would be there too, because he was a fan of Biff's.

Dave's gang could be anywhere. Roddy felt sick when he thought about Dave Boyle and his gang.

The bell rang and everyone pushed their way into the school. He wished he was out there with them, and not stuck up here on his own.

Call a meeting. Yes, that was the thing to do. He needed Biff. She would tell him what to do. He needed Tim too.

He pressed the button beside the mike and said, "Hello?"

HELLO! boomed out across the school.

Hello?

"Will Biff please come to the Head's office at once," he said. "And Tim Tomkins too."

Then he added, "And I want to see Dave Boyle and his gang now. In fact, anyone from Mrs Bigg's class can come along if they want to."

The noise in the school seemed to be getting louder. *The other classes don't know what to do*, thought Roddy.

He pressed the button once more. "Shut up now and listen to me," he told everyone. "Stay in your own classrooms till break. Discuss how you would like the school to be run, and write down some notes. Bring them to my office at breaktime, and I'll tell you what to do next. Thank you."

Biff was the first to get there.

She was followed by Dave Boyle and his gang. Dave was yelling in agony. He said Biff had kicked him where it hurt.

"Shut up and sit down," Roddy said.

Dave stared at him.

"Are you telling me –"

"SIT DOWN!" Roddy yelled at him. "We can't muck about, there are things to do."

"Go on then, big man," Dave said, "while we let you."

His gang grinned and nodded. The whole of Mrs Bigg's class arrived then. They all started to talk at once.

Roddy found a notepad and tried to write down everything they said.

Debbie wanted to know why they could not eat in class. Stewart said school should start at 11 am and end at 2 pm, with an hour for lunch.

A lot of people said teachers mustn't be so sarcastic. Jenny said she couldn't learn anything when people mucked about all the time. A lot of people agreed, but Dave Boyle's gang shouted them down. Danny didn't see why he had been banned from IT just because he had hacked into the school computer system.

Everyone was fed up about not being able to sack the teachers but Sheena said, "Mrs Bigg is all right. She sticks to the rules, but you can see she likes us."

"And Mr Harris is OK, too. He's on our side," said Stewart.

Dave's lot shouted so much that Roddy couldn't hear what the others were saying.

At last Biff yelled, "SHUT UP!"

Then she said to Roddy, "Dave's gang are the real problem. They spoil everything. Lessons are boring because the teachers spend their whole time trying to cope with them. Let's chuck them out."

"You can't, you stupid cow," said Dave. "It's the law. Do you think I'd stay in school if I didn't have to?"

Everyone began to shout at each other.

"LISTEN!" roared Roddy. When they were silent he went on. "What if we take Mr Harris off all other classes and put him in charge of Dave's lot?"

"Great idea," said Biff.

"Harris is a monster," yelled Kevin, who was one of Dave's gang.

"He's tough, but he's fair," another boy said. "When it was snowing last year and my jacket got stolen, he lent me one he had in the back of his car."

At that moment, Mr Rundle put his head round the door. He looked at Roddy and said, "All right, Mr Watt? Anything I can do?"

"Can I hold your hand, Mr Watt?" mocked Dave. "Can I wipe your bum, Mr Watt?"

"Yes, there is something you can do for me," Roddy said to Mr Rundle. "We're going to hand Dave's gang over to Mr Harris, full-time. So could you take them down to Mr Harris's room and give him this note?"

He wrote something on a sheet of paper.

"Tell him the class he's got now can come up here – I'll look after them until we can get things sorted out."

"Right," said Mr Rundle. "I'll take them down now, OK?"

He looked across the room and added, "I'll also take that boy who's drawing on the phone book, and those two girls shouting out of the window. Line up over here by the door, please."

They did what Mr Rundle said. Everyone always did what Mr Rundle said.

"Wow!" said Biff when the door closed. "Peace at last!"

"It's going to stay that way," said Roddy.

He worked harder for the rest of the day than he had ever done in his life.

Biff and the others wanted big changes. They wanted to choose which lessons to attend. They also wanted help for Mr Harris in running his Sin Bin.

They asked for a new rule which said that everyone mucking about in class would be sent to Mr Harris at once. And there would be a new deal with the staff. There would be no chewing gum in class and no cheek. Teachers would mark work the same day and stop making sarcastic comments.

Roddy wrote all this down. He didn't know if it would work or not. But it was worth a try.

At lunchtime, he was too busy sorting out Mr Harris's class to get anything to eat. A pile of notes arrived from all the classes. His assistant came in and said she would type them out for him. She said he needed a break for a coffee and a sandwich.

"You'll have to learn to take it easy," she told him, "or you'll end up barking mad like poor Mr Pimm."

At the end of the school day, Roddy called a meeting to tell the staff about the new rules. Some teachers didn't like them and argued a lot. It all took ages and Roddy was late home. He staggered in and fell into a chair.

"What have you been up to?" his mother asked.

Roddy told her. His mum smiled and said it must be some sort of project. She and Roddy's dad were both teachers. They often talked about things like projects. Roddy was too tired to argue.

He just about got round to eating his tea before going to bed. In the bathroom, he was amazed to see his own face in the mirror. It looked so old and tired.

41

Chapter 5
Mystery

Next morning, Mr Rundle was not waiting outside the flat in his van.

Roddy got the early bus to school and made his way to the Head's office. He felt very tired.

"And where are you going?" asked
Mr Rundle.

"To the Head's office. I mean –"

"No, you're not, son. Not unless you've
been sent for."

"But –"

Roddy looked at the name-plate on the
door, MR RODERICK WATT, HEADMASTER.

"Yesterday, I –"

"Yesterday, we had a new Head. Same
name as you, " Mr Rundle said. "He's still
here today. You took the day off so you don't
know about it. Bunking off school, were you?"

"No!" said Roddy. "You know I wasn't.
I was here. I was working very hard."

Mr Rundle turned round to make sure no-one could hear him. Then he said, "We understand each other, son, don't we? Things will change from now, you'll see. Now, away you go – and don't worry."

Then he knocked on the Head's door and went in, closing the door behind him.

For a moment Roddy saw the new Head sitting behind his desk. His face looked old and tired, just as Roddy's face had done when he saw it in the mirror last night.

Roddy turned away. Biff was coming through the door.

"Hi!" she said. "Where were you yesterday? We've got this new Head. He's great. He's changing everything. And he's got the same name as you!"

"I know," said Roddy.

"How do you know?" she said. "You'd
better get rid of that screwdriver, or you'll
end up with Dave Boyle and that gang in
Mr Harris's room. This Mr Watt's a lot more
strict than the last Head. But he's nice.
We all like him."

"I'm glad," said Roddy.

He set off to the cloakroom. Was he
pleased or sorry? Had he been dreaming
yesterday? Who was the man in the Head's
office with the same name as him?

It was crazy to think that there were
two Roderick Watts.

Could they have been the same person,
just for one day?

The door of Mr Rundle's office stood open. Roddy stopped and looked in. The screwdriver was lying on the table.

A creepy feeling came over Roddy. Mr Rundle had taken the screwdriver off him in the van *yesterday*, on the way to school.

What had Mr Rundle said? "Could be tricky if you were found with it. You being the Head and all."

So yesterday was *not* a dream. Roddy went on into the cloakroom and hung up his jacket. He was smiling. If he could run a school, he could do anything.

He heard the hubbub in the playground. Everyone was waiting for the bell.

The new Head in his office would be hearing it, too. *The best of luck*, Roddy thought. *I gave you a good start, anyway.*

Then he set out along the corridor to take his place in Mrs Bigg's classroom.

Who is Barrington Stoke?

Barrington Stoke went from place to place with his lamp in his hand. Everywhere he went, he told stories to children. Some were happy, some were sad, some were funny and some were scary.

The children always wanted more. When it got dark, they had to go home to bed. They went to look for Barrington Stoke the next day, but he had gone.

The children never forgot the stories. They told them to each other and to their children and their grandchildren. You see, good stories are magic and they can live forever.

If you loved this story, why don't you read ...

Hostage

by

Malorie Blackman

Can you imagine how frightened you would be if you were kidnapped? Angela is held to ransom and needs all her skill and bravery to survive.

4u2read.ok!

You can order this book directly from
Macmillan Distribution Ltd, Brunel Road, Houndmills,
Basingstoke, Hampshire RG21 6XS   Tel: 01256 302699

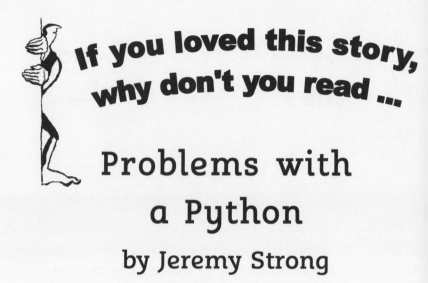

If you loved this story, why don't you read ...

Problems with a Python

by Jeremy Strong

Have you ever looked after a friend's pet? Adam agrees to look after a friend's pet python, but things get wildly out of hand!

4u2read.ok!

You can order this book directly from
Macmillan Distribution Ltd, Brunel Road, Houndmills,
Basingstoke, Hampshire RG21 6XS   Tel: 01256 302699

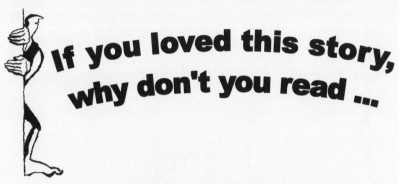

If you loved this story, why don't you read ...

Life Line

by Rosie Rushton

Have you ever told a fib because it was easier than the truth? Skid finds himself in trouble because he tells one fib too many. But how can he tell the truth about his home life?

4u2read.ok!

You can order this book directly from Macmillan Distribution Ltd, Brunel Road, Houndmills, Basingstoke, Hampshire RG21 6XS   Tel: 01256 302699